Operation Achoo!

MAGGIE HYMOWITZ, MD
and SAMUEL HYMOWITZ, DDS

PAGE PUBLISHING, INC.
Conneaut Lake, PA

First originally published by Page Publishing 2020

ISBN 978-1-6624-0875-5 (pbk)
ISBN 978-1-6624-0877-9 (hc)
ISBN 978-1-6624-0876-2 (digital)

Printed in the United States of America

Dedication

To our inspiration for this book, Reiss and Simon.

Written for brave children everywhere
during these unprecedented times.

As the sun began to rise, Gram and Pox popped open their eyes. They pulled off their gooey green blankets and hopped out of bed.

"Hey, Gram, what do you want to do today?" Pox asked.

"Just follow me," Gram said.

2

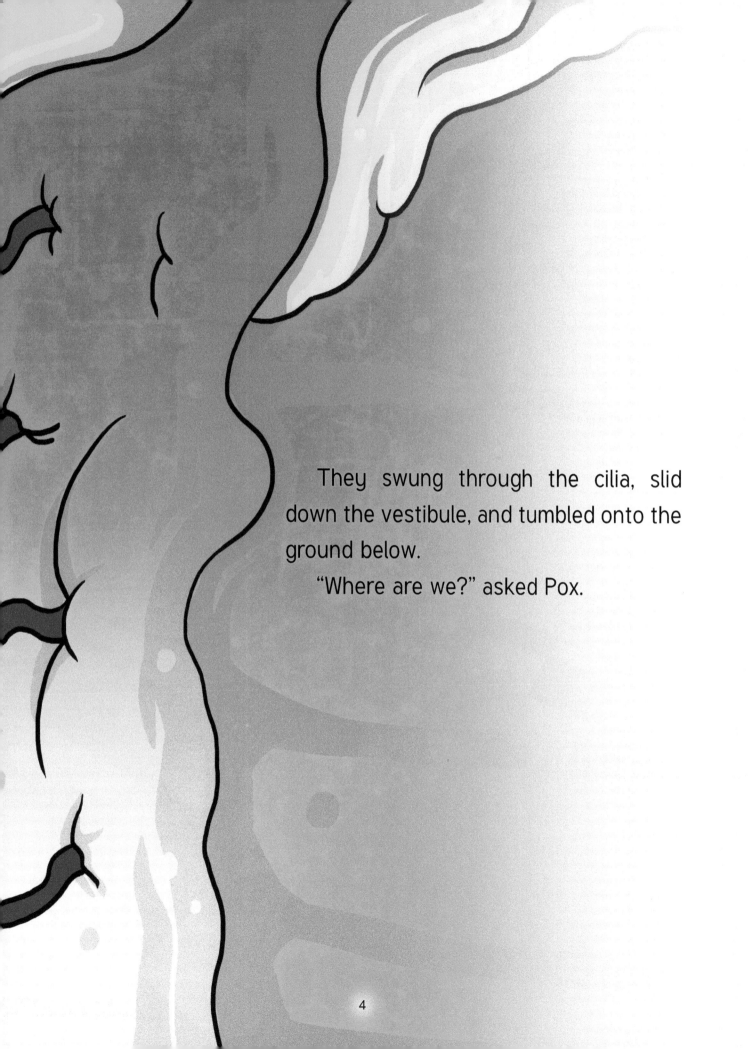

They swung through the cilia, slid down the vestibule, and tumbled onto the ground below.

"Where are we?" asked Pox.

"We are in the bathroom," explained Gram. "Just where we want to be. Let's split up. You climb onto the toilet seat, and I will hang out by the flusher."

Not before long, they heard running footsteps heading for the bathroom. It was Zach.

"Oh boy, am I glad I got in here when I did! I really had to go," he said. Zach lifted the toilet seat.

Gram looked at Pox and said, "Go on...jump!"

With a slight hesitation in his step, Pox leaped onto Zach's hand. Luckily, he landed on all four spikes.

"Phew, I made it," whispered Pox.

When Zach was done, he reached for the toilet flusher. As his hand pushed down on the lever, Gram stretched out his fimbriae and screamed, "Yeehaw!" and soared onto Zach's index finger.

Without wasting a second, Zach ran back outside to finish playing ball with his dog, Tuss. Gram and Pox held on tight and enjoyed the ride.

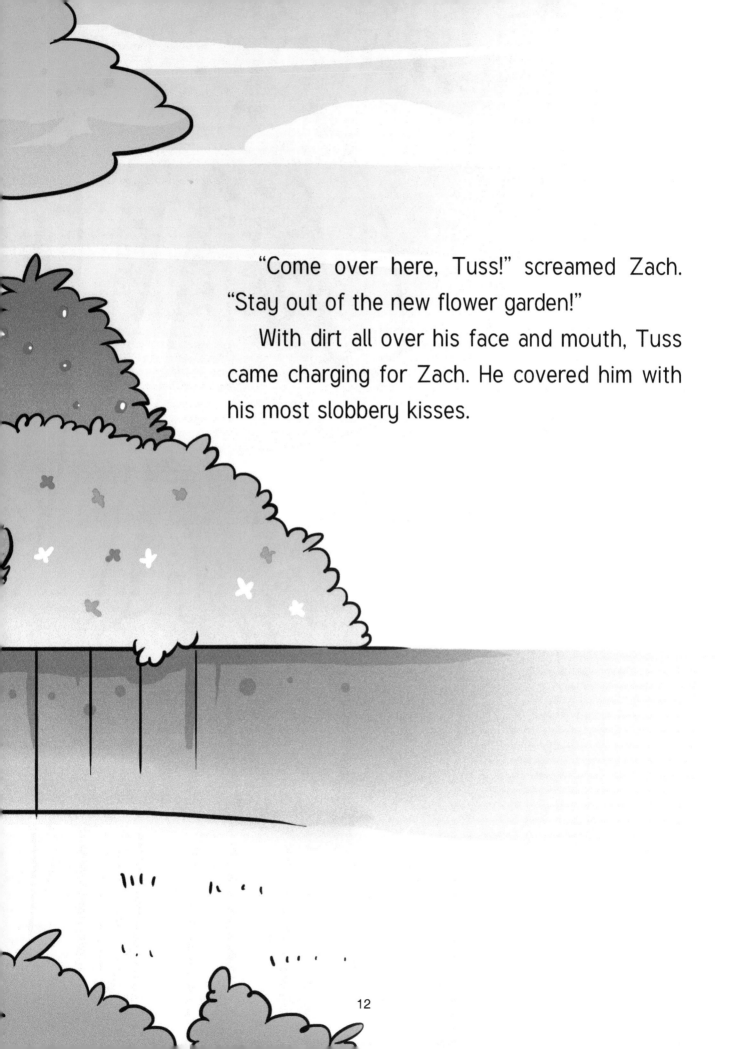

"Come over here, Tuss!" screamed Zach. "Stay out of the new flower garden!"

With dirt all over his face and mouth, Tuss came charging for Zach. He covered him with his most slobbery kisses.

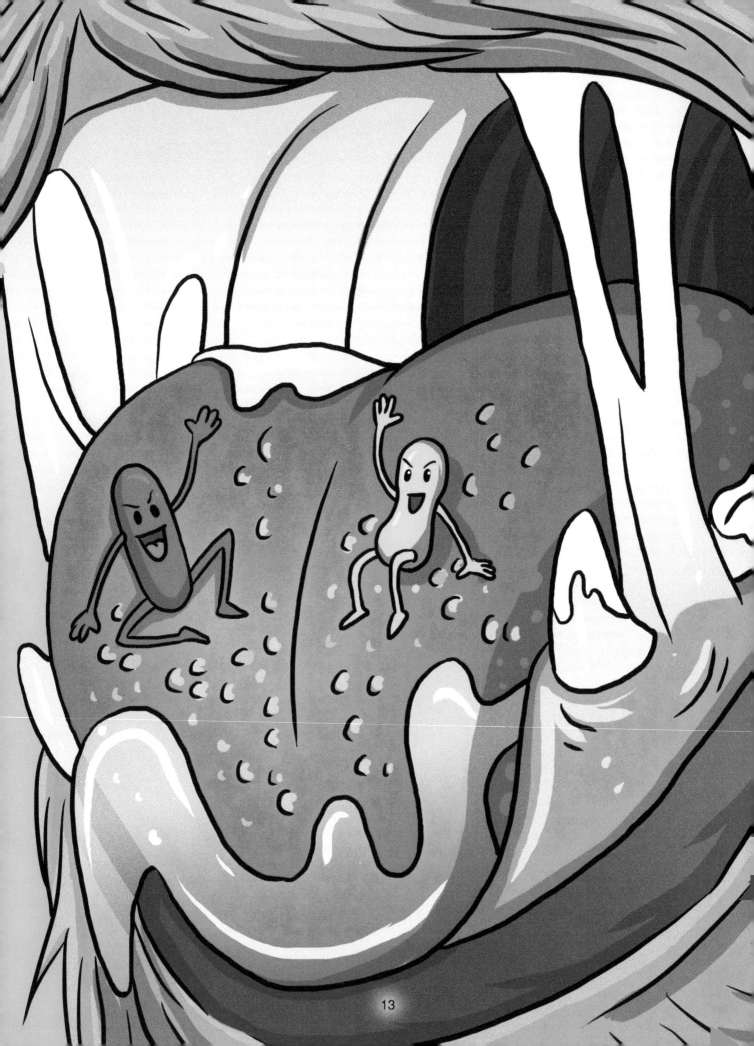

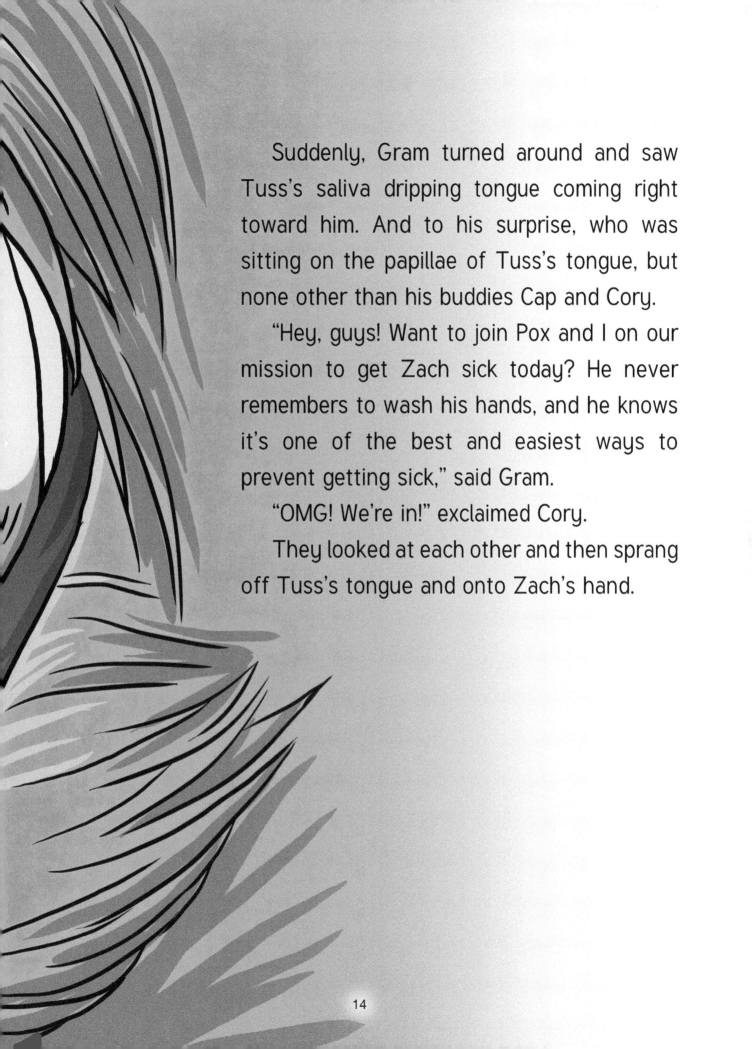

Suddenly, Gram turned around and saw Tuss's saliva dripping tongue coming right toward him. And to his surprise, who was sitting on the papillae of Tuss's tongue, but none other than his buddies Cap and Cory.

"Hey, guys! Want to join Pox and I on our mission to get Zach sick today? He never remembers to wash his hands, and he knows it's one of the best and easiest ways to prevent getting sick," said Gram.

"OMG! We're in!" exclaimed Cory.

They looked at each other and then sprang off Tuss's tongue and onto Zach's hand.

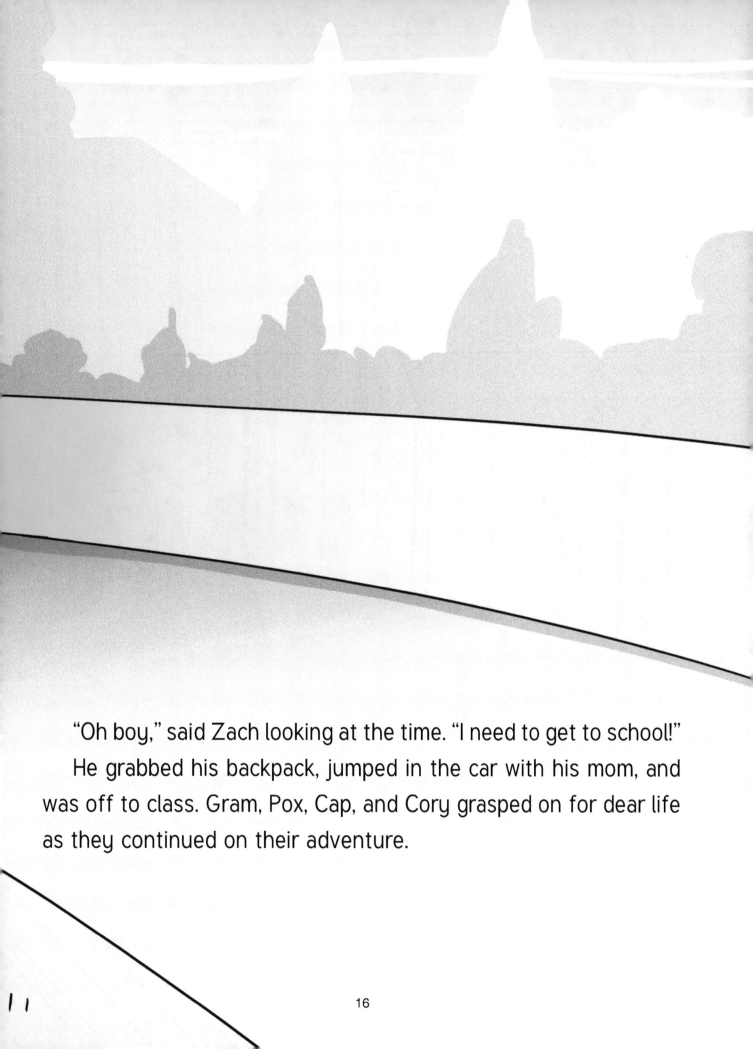

"Oh boy," said Zach looking at the time. "I need to get to school!"
He grabbed his backpack, jumped in the car with his mom, and
was off to class. Gram, Pox, Cap, and Cory grasped on for dear life
as they continued on their adventure.

Late for class, Zach quickly put his backpack in his locker and joined his friends who were already eating a snack.

"Hey, Scarlett!" Zach said.

"Heee...achoo! Achoo! Hey, Zach!" exclaimed Scarlett as they gave each other a high-five. "Want some of my carrots? My mom always packs too many."

"Absolutely!" exclaimed Zach.

As Scarlett leaned over to give him a carrot stick, Cory looked up and spotted none other than Aden, riding the carrot like a cowboy.

"Aden!" screamed Cory. All the germs started jumping up and down with excitement. "Join us on our journey! We are going to get Zach sick!"

"I would never pass up an offer like that," Aden said with a cheeky grin. He stretched out his fibers and leaped toward the others. They all huddled together to make a game plan.

"Okay," Gram said. "On the count of three, when Zach puts the carrot in his mouth, we are all going to jump inside and attach to his throat. Do your best to fight the white blood cells."

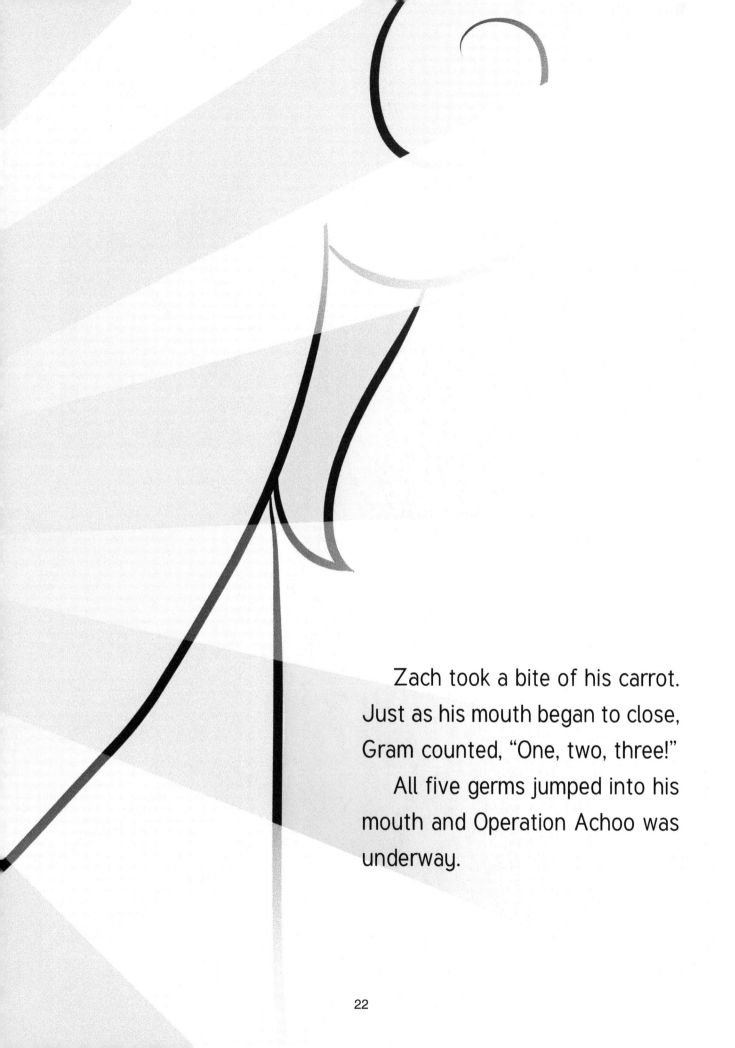

Zach took a bite of his carrot.
Just as his mouth began to close,
Gram counted, "One, two, three!"
All five germs jumped into his
mouth and Operation Achoo was
underway.

The next afternoon, Zach came home from school.

"I'm tired, and I don't really want to eat dinner," he told his mom.

He crept up to his room, got undressed, and crawled into bed.

The sun set, and the sun rose. The glare from the window woke him up, but he could barely open his eyes.

"I feel awful!" Zach screamed. "My body aches and...achoo! Achoo! How will I ever go to school today?"

He was too sick to think. He lay still in his bed.

Then he heard a creak from the door. It was his mom.

"Hi, Mom...I'm sick," whispered Zach.

"I see," she said as she bent down to kiss his forehead. "You went to bed rather early last night. How do you think you got so sick?" she asked.

"Well...what did I do yesterday? I went to the bathroom in the morning, then I played with Tuss—hmmm...did I wash my hands? Oh...I can't remember."

"All right," said his mom. "Then what did you do?"

"I went to school and had a snack with Scarlett who was sneezing and coughing, and...oh man! Did I wash my hands before I shared a snack with Scarlett who was sick? I didn't," he whispered sadly. "I didn't wash my hands at all yesterday."

It all made sense.

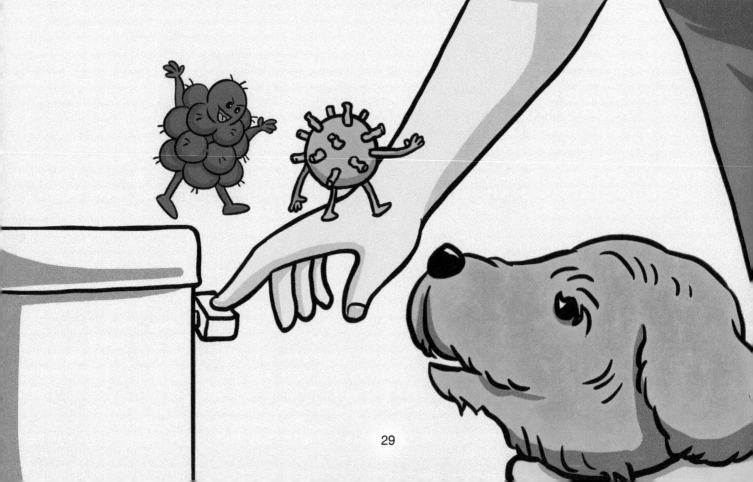

After a few days, Zach was feeling well enough to go back to school. He got out of bed, got dressed, and went to the bathroom. Tuss followed him. Gram, Pox, Cap, and Cory were hanging out in their usual hiding spots.

"There's Zach!" Gram whispered excitedly. "He's looking good. Let's see if we can get him sick again."

As Zach flushed the toilet, Gram and Pox had already grabbed onto his finger. And after one lick from Tuss, Cap and Cory joined them too.

Suddenly the germs heard the sound of water dripping.

"Oh no!" screamed Pox. "Zach is going to wash his hands!"

They all gathered together with the look of fear on their faces. Zach squirted soap on his palms and put them under the faucet.

"Yikes...the waatt—!" garbled Pox.

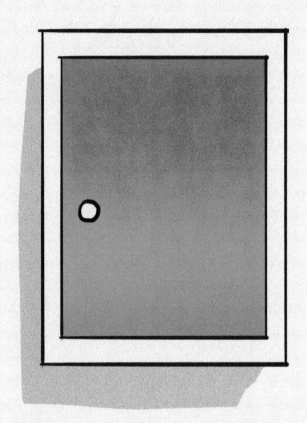

And before they knew it, the germs swirled right down the drain. Zach dried his hands and turned off the sink. He looked in the mirror and said, "I ain't afraid of no germs!" and left for school.

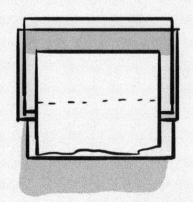

Glossary

Aden: Adenovirus is a virus that can cause infections in different parts of the body like the nose, eyes, and tummy. It can cause fevers, a cough, a runny nose, a sore throat, and body aches. If the virus gets in the eye, it can cause itchiness, tearing, redness, and the eyelids may even be stuck together in the morning! If the virus attacks the belly, it can also cause a tummy ache and watery poop.

Bacteria: Bacteria are tiny living creatures. They are so small that you can only see them under a microscope. Bacteria live all around us, some of which can make us sick and others that can help prevent us from getting sick.

Cap: *Capnocytophaga canimorsus* is a type of bacteria that lives in the mouths of dogs. Most healthy people won't get sick from this type of bacteria, but people who can't fight infections can become ill. This type of infection can cause a person to have a tummy ache, fevers, watery poop, body aches, and a rash.

Cilia: Cilia are little hairs in the nose that help to move mucus into the throat. Mucus is like a gooey jelly (a booger!) that catches germs from the air we breathe. This helps to prevent us from getting sick.

Cory: *Corynebacterium auriscanis* is also a type of bacteria that lives in the mouth of dogs. Most healthy people won't get sick from it, but some people who have other medical problems may get ill. This type of infection can cause problems in the brain, heart, and eye.

Fibers: Fibers are like skinny legs of a virus (Aden) that allow it to search, recognize, and attach to the creature that the virus wants to get sick.

Fimbriae: Fimbriae are like hairs on the surface of a bacteria (Gram) that allow it to attach to other bacteria, human cells, and other objects.

Gram: Gram refers to a color code that is used to group different types of bacteria. There are two groups: gram positive and gram negative. The sign of the bacteria describes the color that they appear when looking at them under a microscope. Gram-positive bacteria are purple, and gram-negative bacteria are red.

Papillae: Papillae are bumps on your tongue (like Tuss's) that give it a rough surface. There are different types of papillae, some of which have taste buds on their surface that allow us to taste foods like chocolate (sweet), pretzels (salty), lemonade (sour), kale (bitter) and soup (umami or savory).

Pox: Pox, also known as chicken pox (varicella), is a type of virus. One can catch chicken pox from coughs and sneezes from someone who has the infection. This virus can cause an itchy rash all over the body, fevers, a sore throat, a headache, and body aches. Luckily, there's a vaccine (a shot that you get at the doctor's office) that helps to prevent us from getting it.

Spikes: Spikes are like little legs of a virus (Pox) that allow it to attach to creatures that the virus wants to get sick.

Vestibule: The vestibule is the entrance of the nose.

Virus: A virus is a tiny germ that needs a host, like a person or animal, to live and grow on and can make us sick.

White blood cells: White blood cells are little fighters that float around in our blood and help to kill bad germs like bacteria and viruses.

Healthy Hands Song
Maggie Hymowitz, MD

Turn on the sink,
Wet your hands,
Scrub with soap
As fast as you can,
Palms of the hands, backs too,
In between the fingers,
We're almost through!
Now we rinse then dry,
It's almost time to play,
We turn off the sink,
and we say,
Hooray!

About the Authors

Dr. Maggie Hymowitz is a New York–based ophthalmologist, educator, and mom. She has a passion for cookie decorating, the New York Yankees, and supporting women's issues. She considers herself "germ conscious," which, with the help of her children's never-ending stuffy noses, inspired her to write this story. *Operation Achoo* is her first children's book, co-authored with her father. She lives in Port Washington, New York, with her husband and two sons.

Dr. Samuel Hymowitz is a retired periodontist and microbiologist with forty-five years of clinical experience. He has performed research in bacteriology, which gives him the expertise to relate to the importance of good hygiene habits and dealing with the challenges of bacteria and viruses in the environment. He looks forward to carrying the message of this book to the younger generation, just as he has for oral health in schools and organizations throughout his professional career. He resides in Manhasset, New York, with his wife of fifty years.

CPSIA information can be obtained
at www.ICGtesting.com
Printed in the USA
BVHW020722191020
590892BV00005B/6